FAMILY
SOLSTICE

FAMILY
SOLSTICE

By
Kate Maruyama

Omnium Gatherum
Los Angeles CA

Family Solstice
Copyright © 2021 Kate Maruyama

ISBN-13: 9781949054323

This book is a work of fiction. Names, characters, places and incidents are either the products of the author's imagination or are used fictiously. Any resemblance to actual events or persons, living or dead, is coincidental.

Library of Congress Control Number: 2020950589

First Edition

For Mom, a cycle-breaking power for good

SUMMER

ONE

Summer is my favorite time. Everyone is driving up and down the east coast visiting, and our house is a must-see, must-stop, never ending cycle of barbecues, boiled corn, laughter, flashlight tag, lightning bugs, and mosquito bites. We live in a small city, Middletown, part way down the Connecticut River. Our City friends from Manhattan and Boston say they're visiting "the country" when they're with us. Our upstate New York and backwoods Pennsylvania or Massachusetts friend say they're visiting "civilization." I like that we live somewhere in between. Whatever they call it, everyone has a good time.

In summer, Mama says, "Open house, open hearts, open life." She is the opposite of winter Mama, with her moods and silences. In summertime, she is hilarious stories, raucous late nights, hugs and encouragement. She's always laden with groceries and stops at the farm stand so that when she gets home, she carries the smell of strawberries, raspberries, corn, peaches, and watermelon into the house with that sapling undertone of wooden crate. She is chopping, grinding, sizzling, cooking fresh things, her honey hair falling out of its ponytail, her peachy-amber tanned face flushed red. She is the hostess, the problem solver and the comforter. This time of year, I can almost forget about Winter Solstice.

Our friends the Campbells are here, Gretchen and Josh are piled in with me and Jeffrey on the string hammock in the back yard, looking up at the maple tree at its mid-summer greenest green. A breeze blows and relieves the stickiness I'm starting to feel where my leg mushes against Gretchen. We don't mind 'cuz we're friends. Josh sits on the wooden bar at the top of the hammock cross legged. Jeffrey's the only sib I can hang with anymore since Martina got too snooty to play all of a sudden. Like Solstice made her too cool for us. Which is funny 'cuz Jeffrey's older. I miss Carl though, he was my favorite. He moved out five years ago when he was seventeen and doesn't even come home anymore.

Gretchen stretches her long pale leg across my lap. It's too hot, but I allow it. The more we can shift position on this hammock, the longer we can stay here. I don't want to move from this spot ever. Soon we'll be called in to wash up, set the table, and it will bring about a nice meal, but for now I want time to stop. Here: the rustling of the maple leaves overhead, the creak of the rope holding the hammock, Gretchen's scratchy-ass razor stubble leg stuck to mine, an aggravated mosquito bite surrounded by the dirt her fingers got there when she scratched it, Jeffrey leaning on me from the other side, but only his head and his shirt touch me because everyone knows sibling skin is gross. And Josh going on and on way too long about some stupid movie he saw I can't remember the title of.

"So then it pulls off her *head* and her face is all *aaaaaaah!* surprised and there is blood squirting, like, everywhere." This is extra ridiculous because he has a maple seed stuck to his nose, the green wing looking like a katydid landed on him and won't leave.

Jeffrey is turning that particular green when he doesn't like hearing about stuff. He can't stand violence and gore, which makes it hard for him to get along with boys. But Josh is stuck with him for the weekend. Unlike the jerks at school, Josh is cool with Jeffrey.

Gretchen and I both say, "Eeeew gross."

And she punches me. "Jinx."

"Seriously it was so cool, They musta used a *pump* or something." Josh is frowning over another seed he is trying to split with his thumbnail to expose its sticky inside to affix somewhere else on his face. This is what passes for activity in July.

Jeffrey says, "Dude, did you see *Corvette Summer?*"

But Josh isn't biting. "Wait. Did you see *The Texas Chainsaw Massacre?*" Josh sits up, shaking all of us, "That was *sick*! Talk about blood. And that chase? Leatherface is scary as fuck."

Jeffrey falls back on the hammock staring at the leaves above him. He'll just tune out and let Josh ramble. It's how he copes.

And Josh does ramble, "Imagine that sick ass family there that whole time. Slaughtering people for however long. And no one knew."

That does it. One more word and I hurl. I whack Gretchen's leg. "All right stickymissstuckle, let's go. This is gonna get gooey."

Jeffrey says, "'Cuz it wasn't bloody enough." He's stuck, though. Josh is on a jag.

Gretchen and I lean forward in unison, tipping the hammock which causes a "heeey" from Josh, but he continues on his grossfest as I feel around under the hammock with my foot to find my other sandal I've left there.

Gretchen and I get up at the same time and jump out of the way before the hammock swings back to hit us. I say, "Let's see what's cooking."

"Starving." She croaks. She's not wearing shoes. She doesn't have a dog at home, so she doesn't know. I tell her and tell her, but I know it takes a step into a fresh poo to really learn why sandals.

"Starving..." Gretchen repeats, more croaky.

"To death..." I croak back in an old schtick that takes us groaning up the back stairs like zombies, scratching at the screen door. I sidestep the stair eaten to pulp by carpenter ants, a forever battle of the family. Not the important one. A shiver of a memory of leafless branches, a gray, gray, winter darkened quiet house, and Mama's closed bedroom door wells up, so I stomp harder up the last stair to bring back summer.

Mama unlatches the kitchen door, hooked in place to keep our fat mutt Gainsly inside, and swings it wide with a squeak that pushes the feeling away.

Gretchen croaks, "Mrs. Massey, we need foooooooood."

Mama gives off waves of fresh basil and garlic as we pass.

I say, "Fettucine?" It's not, really. It's whatever noodles are in the house and she mixes garlic, oregano, and basil into sour cream and shaky cheese, but it's the best thing ever when you're thirteen and growing even though it's too hot out to want pasta.

Mama pecks my head so as not to touch me with her mucky hands. "Mmmhmmm. Can you girls wash your hands and set the table? It's almost lunch."

The bright sunlight from outside on my eyeballs makes the bright yellow kitchen spark dark with white spots for a moment. I wait for my eyes to adjust and see there's a salad of tomatoes and basil and olive oil on the table and what, soda? Orange soda! Mama only buys soda once in a great while. Mrs. Campbell looks tired and was clearly in the middle of telling Mama something serious. She stubs out her cigarettes and smiles at us.

"Gretch, you remember your sunscreen?"

"We were in the *shade*, Ma." She rolls her eyes and huffs into the bathroom.

Mama and I share a knowing smile, because no one in our house would talk back that way. Everything is a little tighter with our family. Closer? We aren't the type to fight or talk back because we have more important things to worry about.

I think about this as we gather at the long table on the sunporch for dinner, all nine of us. The Campbells and the Masseys mixed in. The corn is piled high, the fettucine is never ending, the table glows with the colors of bright orange and green plastic cups, red paper plates and

Mama's giant oilcloth tablecloth in blue with pictures of lobsters all over it. We get real lobsters tomorrow night. Dad has opened all the windows, so it's as good as being outside, minus the mosquitoes.

Against one wall under the windows lies a very old chest Mama says came over on the boat with our family, almost four hundred years ago. On the opposite wall hangs a pub sign, big as a poster, with a ship painted in white on blue that reads Speedwell. Dad was so excited when he scored it at a roadside antique shop in Massachusetts. Our family traces back to the ship Speedwell which is a Big Thing because it predates the Mayflower by, like, twenty years. When he brought it home, Mama thought it was kind of funny because the sign itself is way more recent, eighteensomething, but it livens up the sunporch and the ship is pretty. Our house is filled with old treasures like this. When friends come over, I get puffed up with pride, showing them the Wangunk tribal wampum, beaded baskets, the crazy old wrought iron lock Dad keeps on the mantel attached to a length of chain. Artifacts. Our family. Going way back. Dad always says the Masseys built this country and reaping its benefits is our birthright.

Dad stands up and raises his glass of seltzer water with half a squeezed lime floating in it. He never touches alcohol. Except on Solstice.

He says, "May our prosperity continue, may our friends always surround us, and may our summer be never ending."

We raise our plastic cups in salute. I usually wish really hard for the last part to come true, but this is my year. My first year to battle. I'm worried and excited, but also terrified. After this year, I will know like Jeffrey knows, like Martina knows. I will no longer be the baby of the family. I'll be one of us.

I'm allowed days off training when we have company, so summer provides plenty of breaks. But I have to admit I'm a little relieved when, after lobster night, after a movie day because it was too hot to hang around the house, after staying up too late, sticky with marshmallows from the s'mores, and after sharing everything I know about boys with Gretchen and her with me, the Campbells finally leave. Only five months 'til Solstice. And it's my turn this year. My very first turn.

We can't train when people are here in summer because it's too hot in the attic and Mama said imagine them wondering what we were clomping around about up there anyway. We need the back yard in the evening when the air has started to cool. We aren't all training, that doesn't happen 'til fall, but I want to get ahead, and Martina has offered to work with me a little.

After Mama and Dad are in bed, I worry because Martina has started breathing a bit heavier. I can tell she's going to sleep.

"Martina." I whisper and poke her. I whisper yell, "Martina." But she groans and turns over.

"Nooo." It comes out as a moan.

"You promised!"

"We've got like *months.*"

"You promised." I slip on my shorts and walk over to her bed. I don't totally sit on her. I hover my butt against her shoulder and just press.

"Quit it."

I think she has a crush on Josh. I think she's realizing it's never going to be a thing. Because we are nowhere near our periods yet, and this is definitely a mood.

"It's my year."

She rolls over and sits up, way more awake than I thought she was. She looks at me, one eyebrow dangerously up and cautions, "Take the night off. Enjoy it. This is the last year..." she stops herself. "Just fucking enjoy it, okay? And let me sleep."

There's a finality in her answer I know I can't get past, so I open the door and slip out into the hallway, closing it behind me. Our bedroom door opens on a room we call an upstairs hall, but it's really the size of a living room, with a bannister at the center that wraps into the stairs going down. Mama and Dad's room, Jeffrey's room, and the guest room all open onto the upstairs hall, so you have to be extra quiet.

In the daytime, it's a warm, friendly space with colored sunlight filtering through the stained-glass window at the head of the stairs. At night, it's dark as crazy and the stairwell looks like a giant black mouth you have to walk down into, slowly and around. But this is my year. I've got to be braver than that. And I definitely can't be afraid of this completely harmless part of the house during this completely harmless time of year.

I grab the bannister and follow it down, stepping softly to avoid the squeak on the left at the top, the squeak in the middle halfway down.

This is such a big house, and we are lucky to have it. The youngest member of the family inherits it. Mama was the youngest, which is why we get to live here, and because I'm the youngest, the house will one day be mine.

The house was built in 1902, a big yellow clapboard "revival of Greek revival," Dad calls it. He can go on until your eyes glaze over about the columns (Doric) on the ornate front porch, the gabled attic, the broad lovely windows framed with black slatted wooden shutters. The windows on the first two floors are simple two-paned sashed wood for maximum light. In the attic, they are detailed with intricate panework. It's is only eighty years old, but the inheriting part about the land has been going on since our ancestors—Mama's ancestors—got here all those years ago, when the original house was just a shack on the top of a hill with a lot of land around it. The family sold the land off, but this little quarter acre of it, this house, and Winter Solstice are our birthright. I like how solid and comforting that sounds: birthright.

I creep through the dark front hall and down to the pantry, which is called the pantry even though it's a hallway.

Everything in our house is named kind of wrong, our den is called the study, our attic is called the den, but it's part of what makes it special.

Gainsly sighs in his sleep. I hope he doesn't wake up and start to whine for me.

The kitchen is lit by the dim orange light on the stove and I open the back door, squeaking the back screen open slooowly so as to keep it quiet. I step out onto the porch and survey the back yard. It's one of those funny, overcast, orange-tinged nights where the light pollution means it's never really going to get that dark. It's cooler than my room, so that part is good, but I realize there is no way I'm going to find a stick in this light.

I sneak back in, trying like hell not to squeak, and find my way in the dark, down through the pantry, through the living room into the study, where I feel along the mantel carefully past Dad's prize ship model of the Admiral Colpoys—touch it and you're toast--to the right hand side of the fireplace and down. My hand hits the fireplace tools stand too quickly and there's a rattle. *Shit.* I stop for a second, listening in the dark. I hear nothing until the house sighs.

Our house breathes. You can't hear it in the summer, what with people coming and going and the din of the crickets outside. It's most obvious in winter, but in the summer, once in a while, when things get really quiet, you can tell it's still there.

I'll really freak myself out if I listen too closely. Before I can hear beyond the next inhale, I clamp the poker in my hand and hustle it out the back door. I need a flashlight, but it's up in my room and I don't want to wake everyone by going up there again, so I grab the heavy wooden pepper grinder from the kitchen table as a substitute. I take great care with the back door again and step out into the yard.

I follow the stepping stones carefully down to the part of the yard where Gainsly can't reach. I don't need to add dog shit to this exercise. Poker gripped in the right hand, pepper shaker in the left. The substitute flashlight isn't a big deal, I just need the weight for training, but having a real poker makes me feel more serious, braver.

It's two swishes to the left with the grinder, then stab right with the poker, advance.

Two swishes to the right with the poker, left with the light, advance.

Then three stabs straight forward with the poker and make sure not to look.

Don't look. No matter what you hear or think you see, do not look directly at it. This is very important.

A few rotations, steps forward and it's no longer cool outside, it's sweaty. I try to remind myself it will be cold when I do this for real. It's hard to even imagine in this balmy, mosquitoey air. Jeffrey says at Solstice, it gets so cold you don't even *want* to hold the poker. That you get so tired you don't think you can even swipe again. That's why the training. You have to be able to do this all night.

I practice until my right shoulder burns, until I am so sweaty, I start to stink, until the light pollution sky convinces me it must be dawn.

When I look at my clock radio when I go back to bed it reads only 2:30. How will I keep it up for a whole night? I have to train harder.

The summer is such a beautiful, lazy time and there are some afternoons you're so bored you don't know how you'll manage or you read a book and go to sleep and wake up sweaty and slick because the afternoon has turned from hot to HOT. Or a thunderstorm comes, and you get so excited by the darkening sky and the rain, but it leaves it hotter than it was before. But the sneaky thing about summer is it seems forever and you can get into that dream state, but suddenly it's Labor Day weekend with the last round of guests and Mama makes one big last feast with marinated flank steak roasted on the barbecue, its edges crunchy where Dad let it slide into the charcoal just a little and the strawberry shortcake has turned to peach, but suddenly the sun porch starts to get chilly after dessert and you know school starts Tuesday and like that, it's all over.

FALL

TWO

First day of school, Martina's alarm goes off at the crack. I don't know what about hitting age fifteen has made her so damn high maintenance, but all of a sudden she needs an extra hour for blow drying, for makeup, for tinny music playing out of her Walkman, for laughs or irritated sighs. I think she was saving up all those late sleeping mornings in the summer to punish me now. It's hardly even light out and she's all over the room thunking, flopping, and worse, bitching at me. "How many times I gotta tell you, you can't go through my shit? Now I can't fucking find *anything*." And if it was one, two, even three noises, I could go back to sleep for a bit more. But she's on the side of my bed bouncing it and yelling in my ear, "Don't go through my *shiiiiit*." She prolongs the last syllable into a punishing yell so close to my ear that I feel her wet breath. Gross.

I muffle into my pillow, "Shut up, I couldn't find any navy socks and you don't even have to wear them anymore."

It's not like anything she does, hair, makeup, clothes can make her look any different. The Masseys all look the same. Honey to brown hair, flat blue eyes, bulgy noses that look cute when you're little, too big when you're a teenager. And the thing about Martina, she looks so much like Mama, it's creepy. Only a Mama with heavy blue eye shadow and super pink lipstick.

She lets out an exasperated *ugh* and mercifully leaves the room, closing the door. Now I can finally... Well, damn it. I'm awake anyway.

Mama really does for us on that first day of school. She has us get our stuff together the night before, makes us

lunches, and for breakfast? Pancakes. You have to understand, we are a cereal and English muffin get your own
kind of family. So homemade breakfast is a big deal.

Jeffrey looks a little peaky this morning, worried
around the edges. He got beat up real bad last year at the
high school. It's been going on ever since Carl left. Carl had
only three years on Jeffrey, but he had more substance to
him, more strength. With Carl, you knew you'd be taken
care of, and the kids who knew him wouldn't mess with
Jeffrey. I was sad when Carl left without even saying good-
bye, but when Jeffrey came home in sixth grade with a
black eye and a broken rib, it really pissed me off. Bailing
on us like that, like we'd be fine without him. It's been like
this for Jeffrey at school ever since.

Mama puts a heavy plate of pancakes on the table and
things feel comfy and right, but she won't stop staring at
me. When I catch her, she smiles, and looks away, or gets
to some task or other. Syrup. Dishes. Lunches. Any time
it gets quiet I find her flat, blue, Massey eyes resting on
me once again. I don't remember her ever getting weird
this early before. Usually she doesn't get fully weird 'til
November. But maybe it's because it's my year. And maybe
I didn't notice her looking at Martina that way two years
ago, or Jeffrey three years ago. Maybe you only notice it
when you're the one being looked at.

Every year around November, Mama changes completely, gets quiet, gets introspective, moody. And by
December, she's not so much talking to us. But this is the
first day of school, and there's usually a solid change in the
weather before I can feel this from her. I feel it now, as she
looks at me over her coffee, as she leans on the counter, as
her first day of school smile doesn't seem to reach her eyes.
And I get the sick dread that doesn't usually hit me until
the bottom half of November, after the Halloween candy
is gone. Because however bad Solstice is, Mama's change
around that time of year is worse.

When Dad scoots by her sideways, leans in and kisses her, rubs her shoulders comfortingly, and puts his hand to the side of her face, I know something is up.

Martina and Jeffrey have a school bus, but Dad still has to drive me to school. He drops me before going to the office. Mama says he's a manager at the paper mill, but I'm not entirely sure what that means. The nice thing about Dad is that he isn't about his work as much as he's about his family. All I know is he's home every night around five, hanging out in his favorite spot, the comfy leather office chair at Grandpa's ancient wooden desk in the den. More "Massey treasure," as he calls it. We can be sure to find him there after work if we need help with homework, if we need quiet company, or life advice. I've learned from my friends that the dad who is always around is a rare thing.

When Mama and Dad got married, Dad took the Massey name. I thought it was a hippie thing or something, but later Mama told me it had to do with the house, the land. Dad said, "I married this house." He's really proud of the Massey family history and all of its treasures. The desk was "saved" from "the great fire of 1901," when the house before this one burned down. The family saved only a handful of the furniture, mostly art and other treasures, like that ship on the mantelpiece or the deed for the land that hangs proudly on the wall above it.

Of all of us, I'm the only one of the kids who looks like Dad, skinny head, long body, but I'm colored like Mama and my sibs and have that distinctive Massey nose. Dad is super pale, his noise is pointy and his eyes are a muddy brown.

I grab my lunch and newly minted backpack, put on my new shoes, and slide into the old Subaru that smells like sunburned Naugahyde. Dad starts up the engine and we're headed down the hill when he says, "So, how you feeling about seventh grade, Shea?"

I groan.

He knows better. He laughs. "Okay then. You know what your sister says."

"Sucks and then it's over." I wiggle my toes around in my new school shoes. Stupid regulation loafer things, but they're more comfortable than last year's pair. I went from kid sizes to grownup sizes in one summer flat. Grownups have it all, even more comfortable shoes.

"Right." He's drumming on the steering wheel, in a good mood this morning.

I'm not about to let that good mood sit. "Doesn't help much on the first day of a whole year of suck."

"A school year."

"Still."

Dad says, "In a few months, honey, all of these daily nuisances won't be as big a deal. I promise. You're part of something so much bigger." He reaches his hand out and grasps the back of my neck like he does when he's proud. I always thought it was like a mama dog grabbing her puppy by the scruff. "I'm so thrilled for you, Shea, and everything you'll be stepping into."

That's nice and all, but he's been saying this stuff for years now and it doesn't take away the fact that I'm headed into seventh grade, which is still gonna suck. Martina and Jeffrey didn't seem especially happier after they'd fought on Solstice, in fact Jeffrey went to his room and didn't come out for a week. I don't think it's the cure-all Dad makes it out to be.

The Subaru does a slight lift and leaves my stomach as it sinks down, going over a rise on the right side of High Street where it splits to go up a hill. The feeling is so familiar and yet we don't take this road much during the summer, so it brings school feelings back to me full force.

Martina says junior high kids don't stop being major assholes 'til eighth grade when they realize they're all leaving. My main torturers, Jimmy and Suzanne had whipped themselves into a frenzy by spring of sixth grade, making my every day a living hell. Right now, I'd give anything to be back at home, surrounded by family friends, up to my eyeballs in buttered corn.

Dad rubs the back of my head and drops his hand back to the steering wheel. We ride along for a moment under the green leaves, the gold light promising a change. Mama's breakfast weirdness comes back to me.

"Dad?"

"Mmm?

"Is Mama okay?"

"Yeah, why do you ask?" his response comes quickly, it feels like it's pre-written.

I look at him. I catch a flicker of worry cross his face and then he firms into a smile and raises his eyebrows at me Groucho Marx style, like we're having a totally different conversation.

I'm not about to drop it. "She seemed a little more November than September this morning."

He breathes in, weighing what he's about to say.

I hate that. I wish grownups would just say the thing.

"You're the baby, you know. The youngest. She might be thinking about that."

I'm not sure what I'm supposed to say back.

He says, "Same spot as last year for pickup?"

Mama's sentimental. So, I guess that's a thing. But the way Dad changes the subject so swiftly, I can't help but think there's something he's not telling me. In addition to the other things no one tells me. At least this is my last year of not knowing.

Before I have a chance to think about it, we pass the supermarket and the school looms on the hill. I'm not letting the dumbasses at school get to me this year. I have more important things to worry about.

Carl doesn't come home anymore. I was only eight when he bailed. I loved him and worshipped him and when his friends were over, I sat outside his door, listening, pining, wishing they'd let me in to listen to albums or laugh or smoke. They were so cool.

When Carl was home alone, he'd let me come in and lie on his floor and ask him questions. Sometimes he'd tickle me or show me something cool or tell me things about life. Sometimes he'd draw me a picture of anything I'd ask. Skeletons, trees, dragons. I can't remember any of the specifics now, but I do remember it was after Christmas. But more likely after Solstice that Carl started to change and didn't talk much and didn't have his friends over anymore. He was hardly here at all, and two nights after his high school graduation, he was gone, everything cleared out of his room.

No one could give me a real reason why. I cried and cried until finally Mama, tired of it all, said. "Honey, you grow up and move away. It's just what happens." She meant to say it kindly, but it came out more as a *shut up already*.

Later, when I asked Dad, he sighed long and hard and said, "Sometimes growing up hurts so bad you leave the place you did it." I didn't ask more because I knew Dad had left his own family. For *reasons*. The kind of reasons he didn't talk about and it felt like it would hurt to ask.

Every time we sat down to a meal, I thought of Carl and the mythical Toby and I don't even remember him at all. Toby was five years older than Carl, and whenever I asked where he was, Mama got super quiet and Dad gave answers like, "traveling the world," or "I hear he's in grad school now." Toby became this free spirit who wrote postcards once in a while. Part of me wondered if they'd all made him up, if they were having one over on me.

When I was ten, I had an obsessive need to write letters to Toby and was going to ask Mama for his address and some stamps when Martina said, "God, don't you *get* it? We don't talk about Toby. You can talk about Carl, but we don't talk about Toby. Can't you see it hurts Mama?"

All I needed was to have the words said, then every time I looked at Mama, I saw this in her. When Toby came up after that by accident, Mama's face would crumple or she'd leave the room suddenly, or she'd get real quiet. One time at Thanksgiving, I said, "I always feel like there's someone missing at Thanksgiving," and Mama's mood went full December, and she went to bed for three days.

Dad got serious with me and said, "I want you never, ever to talk about Toby again, do you understand?"

That's when I began wondering if maybe Toby wasn't in grad school or traveling the world. If something worse happened, like drugs, or prison. Kathy diGirolamo's brother was a junkie now, hanging out on Main Street and her family kind of ignores him. I wonder if Toby is someone like that.

Toby's only presence in the house is in a family photo that hangs in the back hallway upstairs, the four kids with me in Mama's belly at the beach. He stands in the back with sandy blonde hair and chunky brown glasses like all the writers wore in that decade. A turtleneck that is likely an awful color and those stripey pants. So much is hair and glasses and squint that I can't really get a good sense of him. Does he have blue eyes like me or brown like Jeffrey's and Dad's? Was he funny like me, brave like Carl, or serious and wimpy like Jeffrey? Were he and Carl close? Were they living together somewhere now? These questions nag at me every so often. There's a part of me that wonders if, once I'm shown the other side of Solstice, I'll know the answers. But even Martina isn't telling.

Carl and Toby grew up and left. But I'm not going to grow up and leave. Because I'm the youngest, I get the house. I'll be in charge of carrying on with Solstice. Maybe then I can convince Carl to come home for holidays.

This coming Solstice is like a mysterious corner I'll turn. Laid out in front of me will be the rest of my life.

The Saturday after the first week of school, we help Dad take all the cushions off the patio furniture and move it all into the garage for winter. Martina sweeps the patio, which has only a few leaves, some spent matches, a stray sparkler, and a citronella candle that has pooled with rain so long it's likely unlightable, the detritus of a summer totally gone. But this year, my heart skips with the preparation. This year is my year to work with Dad, one on one.

It's not like I haven't trained before, but I've been the baby in training for so long, when the older kids were the special ones getting ready for their turn. Your first time comes when you turn thirteen. I honestly thought Mama was going to put it off was for another year because I'm a cusp baby. She kept me out of preschool an extra year because, being born in October, I was going to be the youngest in my class. She said I just wasn't ready. But here I am, training for Solstice before my thirteenth birthday.

It makes no sense to me how we were just out here for Labor Day and it was hot and mosquitoey. But now, at ten in the morning on the Saturday after, the light is a totally different golden, the sky a brilliant blue, and there's a slight chill in the air from the night before. The crickets have moved from a constant din to isolated chirping. In another month they won't be there at all.

Dad gives me his softer, hopeful look as I assume the stance. Is he being gentler with me? He always barked orders at Jeffrey when it came time for his solo training, made him cry a few times. Come to think of it, he barked at Martina too. She didn't cry, though. She's tough.

"All right?" He asks.

"Tell me." I say.

"Swipe twice left, stab once."

I do the moves before he can get them out in words. He raises his eyebrows, impressed. "You've been sneaking around on me, haven't you?"

I flush. "I didn't...it wasn't sneaking. It was preparing."

"Good girl."

My chest puffs with pride. Dad is hard won and when you win his approval, it's like being named captain of something, it's like being king of the afternoon.

He corrects my elbow position only once and has me take a swipe at him with a stick which he ducks.

"Does *it* duck?" I say.

This flusters him. "You have to. You know I can't. I'm just trying to make you ready for anything."

The not talking about anything before they send you down into the basement makes all of this so hard. I argue and argue that how am I supposed to know what I'm fighting unless I know what I'm fighting? My arguments are always met with a smartass comment from Martina or Jeffrey. That weighted, "Oh you'll KNOW, you know," or, "None of us knew, why should we start telling you now?"

I never. Ever. Get a straight answer.

So to Dad I just say, "I know, no questions, only knowledge."

"Attagirl."

Okay.

We train a full half hour more than he thought we would. I get sweaty, he gets sweaty, we laugh. I look up only once to see Mama in the upstairs window looking down. She holds a cup of tea and is too far away for me to read her expression. Usually, this early in the season, she might call out something encouraging. But this time, she just raises her chin in greeting and disappears inside the house.

That night for dinner is hangaburgers on English muffins. They're medium rare and soak the muffin so it falls apart. They've never been so delicious before. I can't remember which kid started calling them hangaburgers, but it was the family word after that.

I ask for a second burger and actually get one. It's not so bad being golden this year.

Unprompted by anything, Dad watches me eat and says, "I'm not worried about this girl. Nope, not at all."

Martina and Jeffrey flash surprise and then glare at me jealously, somehow managing to maintain that look of *you don't even know*.

I'm finally, *finally* going to be on the other side of that look.

THREE

Martina's first Solstice battle made me so nervous I felt like I was going down there with her. She was up all night the night before and I thought I heard her crying. I said, "And you're gonna tell me, right?"

She whispered back a little too angrily, "I told you I would."

"I know, but Jeffrey never told us."

She said, "I think it's just rude keeping us from knowing what we're going into. I think it's better a person should be prepared." She reached across to my arm and squeezed saying, "I want better for you little sister." I didn't like how, even just eighteen months older, she was always so superior, but right then, it felt good to be taken care of.

Martina's Solstice dinner was early as usual. At noon, Mama came out of her room for the first time in a week and went about the business of making dinner. It was such a different thing than our other holidays: Fourth of July, her face glowed and laughed with summer, Halloween she beamed and flushed at her pumpkin carving party when we could invite all of our friends and there were stacks of popcorn balls, candy and "Monster Mash" playing over and over, Thanksgiving she was subdued but full of warmth, filling the table, giving lots of affirming hugs. Come December, we knew better than to talk to her too much.

At noon on Solstice, she started bustling around the kitchen, and it was the one time we were discouraged from helping. She made a pork roast and potatoes and a green salad. Our glasses were brimming with milk and that was the only night a small tumbler of whiskey sat at Mama and Dad's places at the table.

On Solstice when I was five, I was sent to bed early with a pile of books, ordered to use the attic bathroom and not to leave my room for *any, any reason*. At that age, I thought the whiskey was a special grownup treat. When I was big enough to sit Solstice, with Dad and whatever kids were left at the kitchen table, I understood the whiskey was more like medicine for the evening. Like the cocoa Mama made us before she went off to bed.

Solstice dinner was served at 4 pm, half an hour before sunset.

We ate quietly, and then Dad suited up Martina. The catcher's breastplate was a little big on her, so Mama pinned it up at the shoulders to close the gap near her clavicle. "We can't have any vulnerable parts out, that leaves her chest wide open."

Martina's eyes widened behind the mask in the first fear I'd seen her show outright. And when Dad got out the duct tape to fix the flashlight to her hand, she jerked with the pulling and there might have been tears in her eyes. I looked away so she wouldn't know I saw.

The second time he went down, for you went into rotation if it wasn't your first year, Carl had a sense of seriousness and bravado about him. Jeffrey cried every time it was his turn and his first time, he whined like I hadn't heard since he was a kid. The first time was scary for anyone. This was something we understood.

Mama stirred hot chocolate on the stove while Dad lifted the 2x4 off the brackets where it hung blocking the basement door. He opened the door, releasing its musty, cool dirt odor. He was always very businesslike with whichever kid was going down there. Hands on the shoulders, pat on the back, no hugs. It was weird, 'cuz Dad was ordinarily a very huggy guy.

Martina's year, I scooted into my seat at the kitchen table early and clenched my eyes shut when she went down.

I don't know why, but I couldn't watch her disappear on me. I stood and watched Carl, then watched Jeffrey when Dad had to give him a final shove through the door, but with Martina it was different. A sister thing? I looked up only when I heard Dad put the bar back in its brackets.

We spent the night at the table waiting and listening, at first as the furnace kicked in, fighting that cold, and later, to those horrible noises, the roars and growls and clanks coming up from below. I knew the training, I knew we were fighting something, and when Martina came up that next morning with the dawn, she would tell me. I would be prepared. I wouldn't have to be scared like her, or at least I would know what I was scared of.

Mama never could sit through it. Every time, she made us our cocoa, poured a little more whiskey into Dad's, served us, pecked us each on the head with a dead look in her eyes and went off to bed. She made sure to be up early the next morning, waiting for her child to reemerge. But the long night was too much for her.

This time when Mama went to bed, with Martina down in the maw of I don't know what, anger forked in my belly. Here we were, standing watch for her, worried about our sib and Dad was toughing it out watching over us. Why did Mama get to go to bed? Why did she get out of this shit? 'Cuz she got more depressed? How was that fair?

Dad was always looking after her. He was the protector. The knight in shining armor, I guess. I made up my mind then and there that when I grew up, whoever I married wasn't going to let me puss out of life things. We'd fight shit together.

I fell asleep somewhere around midnight, my face down on the table. I didn't even notice when Dad carried me to bed. I just know I woke up with the weird light on the ceiling the next morning and sat up suddenly in bed. Everything was bright and strange. It had *snowed*. I looked out the window, excited, and was about to call Martina's name when I remembered.

I looked over at her face bathed in that bright light and a bandage flashed white on her forehead. There she slept, next to me, her eyes working on her dreams, and like that, she knew.

The morning after Solstice, the family woke whenever they did. The darkest thing had lifted from the house and you could find people zonked out all over, sometimes in front of the television. It was quiet again, that increasing breathing before Solstice gave way to the simple quiet of the furnace kicking in every so often to keep us warm. There was leftover whatever in the fridge and whatever canned food or pasta in the cabinet. Mama got up somewhere after lunch and started puttering over the Christmas decorations, already moving on. It felt like the pressure released from a can of nuts, the *pfff*, and we all could breathe a little more and move around a little easier. And best of all, we got Mama back.

Whoever fought the night before got the first of everything; they were allowed to be king for a day. They had the pick of the TV channels, the pick of the treats in the cabinet, the best chair that sat right in front of the TV. This was done without discussion or argument.

Martina would *not* wake up. I snuck down and grabbed breakfast and went back to our room to stare at her, waiting. I pretended to read like five different books and stared at her some more. They say if you stare at a sleeping person, they'll eventually wake up.

On Christmas Day, I'd sometimes throw stuff at her because I wasn't allowed downstairs 'til she was up, but this was different.

Around noon Mama came up with a sandwich to check in on her. She brought the plate over to me with a warm smile, her eyes weary, but alive once again. She kissed me on the head and then stood over Martina a moment. She held her hand just over Martina's hair and pushed her bangs off her bandage. She put a glass of water and two aspirin next to her bed and then snuck out with a conspiratorial wink. I guess she thought I just being a good sister, looking after Martina. She didn't know I was waiting to be told the secret. I had a twinge of guilt, but screw that lady who hadn't even sat up in the kitchen. What was it Mama was making us do every year?

The first time Mama told me about Solstice, I was five. I was curled up on her lap Christmas Eve watching the lights on the tree and squinting until they spun out starlike in my eyeballs. Bing Crosby was singing about a white Christmas but it was weirdly warm that year, so it didn't look like a white Christmas was going to happen. I'd been super disappointed about that the minute before, but something wasn't leaving me.

"Mama?"

"Mmm?" She had eggnog breath. It wasn't alcoholy eggnog, it was the kind without and she smelled sweet and comfy and I had one of those Mom moments where you wanted to cry just 'cuz you love her so much and the lights are so beautiful and Santa is coming. But soon it will be over, and you will miss it.

I said, "There was a lot of noise last night and Martina wasn't in her bed and the house was breathing big and I went to find you, Mama, but you were sleeping and Daddy wasn't with you and what was happening, Mama? What happens when the house gets like that? Why is it so *angry*?"

Bing Crosby made the bells ding, and Mama's whole body got unsoft for a minute, hard like a chair. Then she wrapped her arms around me super tight and kissed my hair, and she said, "Baby, it's time for you to join us in the family story. It's a rich piece of who we are, and there are parts you aren't going to understand, but that's okay. When you're ready to learn all the things, we'll tell you, okay?"

Her voice got all reverent like when she was telling me about our grandmother I never met or when she was reading *Arabian Nights*. This was important. And with her tight squeeze around me, the lights glowing, and "Holly Jolly Christmas" starting, I felt safe and warm when she told me about Solstice. She told me how this was a very special part of our family ever since we first came to this undiscovered land almost three hundred years ago. How we claimed the land and built this country into greatness. How we are so grateful for this house and all it gives us, the warmth, the friends, the maple tree out back, the bounty it brings forth every year, so we can live and have these beautiful Christmases and grow all big and strong. But we had to do something for the house every year. A big, brave thing I would understand when I was older, and I would become part of that grownup thing that my siblings were doing for us. She told me how our family had been in charge of this very important thing, this safeguarding, for all our people for a very long time. But this year, because I knew, this was a very special year, because I'd get to start training with the big kids.

She bundled me closer, squeezing my legs around me and holding my whole body in a comfy ball saying, "You, my little bug, you are the most special because you are the youngest. One day, when you are grown like Mama, you're going to have a very special thing to do for the house." She kissed my head and whispered into my ear the thing she whispered into each of our ears when she got us alone, "I love you most." But there was something about how she said it that made me think that maybe, just maybe, she did.

That fall I got my first stick.

Martina finally woke up sometime after two. She blinked at the light, squinting and sat up slowly with a sharp grunt because she was sore. I didn't say anything. You had to let just-woken Martina get her bearings, or she'd hit you.

She drank the whole glass of water down and put it on the table. Her hand flew up to her bandage and she touched it and winced. She swung her feet onto the floor and got up.

"Martina."

She held her hand up, "one minute," and padded into the hall. I heard the bathroom door slam and waited for the flush. After the flush, I waited as she walked back toward the bedroom, but stopped just outside the door. Looking at the snow? Would she go downstairs? Was she gonna faint?

She came back into the room and her chin was set. I didn't want to believe her expression, but her words confirmed it. "I'm not. Saying. Anything."

"You promised." It came out more whiny than I wanted but *come on.*

"I shouldn't have promised. You just gotta wait."

"I *can't* wait. What about everything we talked about. Isn't it better to know? Wouldn't it be better to know?"

She sat down on the bed, pulled her knees into her chest and buried her face in them. I pushed the plate with the aspirin on it toward her. She looked up at me, super serious and said in that damned *knowing* voice. "Trust me, kid." *Kid?* We were only one year apart in school. "It's better *not to know.*"

With that, she flopped down in her bed and pulled her quilt over her. And I was left the odd man out for two more years.

FOUR

Halloween is two weeks after my thirteenth birthday. Dad is grinning and keeps saying, "Nope, nothing to worry about with this one. She's strong." To the point where it starts getting on everyone's nerves.

I have him alone one night on our way to Pizza Palace to pick up our weekly order of one garbage pizza, two pepperoni pizzas, and one plain. I say, "Um Dad?"

"Yeah, kiddo?"

"I love that you have confidence in us and everything, but maybe, just can you um. Can you stop complimenting me so much on how I'm doing? It's really pissing off Martina."

He laughs for real and then turns nervous and he says, "Oh. Heh. Yeah, I didn't think about that. I'm just." He stops for a moment, "I'm just so proud of how you manned up to this, you know?"

"That's kinda sexist."

He laughs again, "Your mother's daughter. Okay, you grownupe'd up to this. Like, you're ready."

"Is it different from anyone else?" Seems to me Martina was pretty brave about things. Everyone who came before seems pretty brave to me.

"Are you kidding? Carl was totally terrified. He cried the night before Solstice. You don't remember?"

"I was like three, Dad."

"When it came time, he manned up, but whoah, he was pretty worked up leading up to it."

"Dad."

"Sorry. I know. I'm just saying. And Jeffrey." He rolls

his eyes. He knows I know Jeffrey's a total wimp. I can still hear that last yelp as Dad shoved him through the door and barred it behind him.

Dad pulls into the parking lot and I smell that gorgeous pizza tinge to the air. My mouth starts watering. With all the training, I'm always hungry these days. He says, "You're a good kid, Shea. Don't let anyone tell you different. You're a solid..." I can tell he's rewriting wherever his fifties brain has gone. "You are an excellent human being."

"We'll make a feminist of you yet, Dad."

On the way home, the pizzas, so toasty and delicious smelling, weigh my lap down, making my thighs sweat through my jeans. It's a singular feeling, the cold night, the warm pizzas, the smell filling the car. A whole different animal in the spring. I have to ask. "And Toby?"

"What?" He didn't hear it and then he does hear it and reprimands. "Shea."

"Was Toby brave?"

"Shea, what have I told you."

"Dad."

He doesn't answer and we drive another half a mile before he says, "Toby was the bravest of all. But you are not to mention him ever, especially in front of Mama, okay?"

"Okay." This doesn't jive with my idea of Toby burnt out somewhere in a different town. I say, "Does Toby..."

He cuts me off in a terrifying voice I rarely hear him use, he says, "Do you understand me?"

"Yes, sir."

I sit back, no longer hungry, shamed that I even brought it up.

When I was very small, it was the third rainy afternoon in a row one summer and I snuck up to the attic where I heard Carl, Jeffrey and Martina playing. I wasn't allowed up there because there were roofing nails sticking out of the wood and lathe ceiling and Mama worried I'd bonk my head and get tetanus, but what was I supposed to do for three days alone in my room? I stood on the third step down looking through the railing, the floor of the attic level with my nose. The attic was bare warm colored wood, floor and slanted ceilings done in wide planks. It had windows all around, and was usually bright, but today was the kind of gray that made everything dingy.

In the corner on the right was a fort made of cardboard boxes full of stuff. Carl had pulled an electric lamp in there and run the cord into Toby's room. Toby's room was just off the attic and had the coveted clawfoot tub. Now that he was gone, no one was allowed in there. But I was the age when I started to notice that the older kids didn't always do what they were supposed to.

Martina had a strain in her voice when she said, "It's too tight." Her voice came from the other side of the attic, so I slid silently across the stair and peeked out through the other railing. The rain was extra loud, fat, steady pattering on the uninsulated roof.

Carl said, "You're there forever, it's gotta be tight."

Martina said, "I don't like this game."

Jeffrey said, "It's a very important game and even if Carl won't tell us why, I think we have to do it."

Martina was tied to the chimney, which rose up through the center of the house from the front hall. She looked so weird in her aqua shorts and stripey T-shirt, her hair still bed mussy, cords tied around her. She squirmed to get free.

Carl stood over her, hands on his hips. He said, "Martina, it is your duty to protect us all. And to protect us all you must be bound." He sounded somber, important.

Martina said, "It's hard to breathe. Jeffrey get me out of here."

He said, "We get the point, Carl. What's the next part?"

Carl said, "We have to be strong. We have to know this, and we have to leave her."

"You're not gonna. No, Carl, c'mon." There was an edge of tears in her voice.

"It's not funny, Carl, let her go." Jeffrey had tears in his voice, too. I didn't know why my favorite brother was making everyone so miserable.

Carl started walking toward the stairs and I gasped and stepped down a step, ducking below the edge of the floor.

Martina said, "I'm going to tell Mama."

"Mama knows. Everyone knows." His voice was heavy and horrible.

Jeffrey said, "Shut up. You're a total creep." He leaned in and started untying Martina.

Carl said, "Fine. But you don't know. You don't *know*." He stormed right past the staircase into Toby's room and slammed the door.

Martina was crying. "He's just so *mean*. He's never been downright *mean* before."

Jeffrey cleared his throat and said, "Let's go get some ice cream."

"Promise me you won't get that mean when it's your turn." Her arms were free, and she pulled her knees up to her chest.

"I think Dad got rocky road."

"Promise me, Jeffrey."

In a very unJeffreylike move he pulled Martina in for a hug. In a very unMartinalike move, she let him. Jeffrey said, "Promise."

I skibbled down the stairs as quickly and quietly as I could before they could catch me. I don't remember if I made anything of it at the time, I just remember thinking the older kids were weird and I didn't like Carl so much that day.

I put this away in that file of weird family moments when the olders were discussing things. But for some reason, talking about Toby with Dad brought it back. It was a piece of Solstice I couldn't make fit.

Thanksgiving we sometimes have the Mullins over, but they took this year to go on a trip to Italy. Who even does that? So it's just the five of us which means it's a little harder to ignore Carl being gone, the impending winter, the loss of Mama, which is so hard every year, and the overall pall, the threat that comes over the house. Mama goes through the motions and makes us roast duck stuffed with wild rice and with orange sauce and three kinds of pie which comes out to more than half a pie a person, but when you're eating lemon fluff pie made of frozen cream and pecan pie and pumpkin, you don't so much care that it's too much food, especially when there isn't a whole lotta conversation at the table.

Mama says Grace, and it's familiar, thanking God for all our blessings and allowing us to live here and allowing us the goodness of the house and I think she'll get straight to, "Thanks for Solstice and all the bounty it yields," but she chokes up this time and looks right at me and says, "And thank you God for Solstice. We know that it's sometimes harder than we think we can manage, and sometimes we have to give more than we want to." *What does that even mean, am I going to lose a finger or something?* "But we understand its importance in the larger scheme of things, we understand why we do this, and we understand when sacrifices must be made. It is our birthright."

Sacrifices? Oh shit, is there a dying animal part of this? Am I gonna have to kill a goat? I shuffle through all the past Solstices with all my siblings in my head and the only one where there was any blood was when Carl came out of the basement with an enormous gash in his arm. I don't think he cut himself. Mama sewed it up and ordered antibiotics from her doctor cousin on the phone. She said we couldn't trust it to the hospital. It was weird at the time and I remember this because that year I read the Richard Scarry book about hospitals and what they're for and there were definitely stitches involved but there was Mama with the blue thread sewing up Carl's arm while Dad poured himself a second glass of whiskey.

All of this blows through my head as Mama stands,

staring into space and we aren't sure if the toast is done and I say, "Mama?"

And she says, "I love you so much, Shea. We are two of a kind."

And she leaves it there.

The next morning, I get up before it's even light out and head to the attic with the poker and a flashlight. The windows are black and the single lightbulb in the ceiling casts an orange glow in the chilly uninsulated space, its corners black with shadows. I tell myself the dark and the cold is good for training, but I know the warm, wood dust smells of the attic are a far cry from the cold, musty cellar.

I swipe, swing, and thrust. I fight through the fatigue of turkey and pie in my muscles and forge on for two hours straight before Dad finds me and calls me down to breakfast.

WINTER

FIVE

The day before Solstice is a Monday and Mama lets me take off school. She makes Dad take me out to buy me a nice dress for Christmas day; I outgrew the one she got me in September on sale. I'm growing out of everything. My pants are all highwaters.

It's so weird, shopping with Dad. Mama usually does that with us. Shopping at all this close to Solstice is weird anyway. We just don't do that. I think maybe Mama's getting me out of the house so she and everyone else can like, I don't know, throw me a surprise party? Cook me a special homemade something 'cuz it's my year? There's never been anything like that in the past, but being thirteen means playing scenarios out in your head that can or can't happen in equal measure. It's no more weird that this occurs to me than my fantasizing about having a loft apartment in New York where I can have my friends over and have a real hanging chair like the ones at that rich person's house we visited five years ago—it's a white plastic pod that hangs from the ceiling by a rope and you can turn it around if you don't want to face the room.

Dad's at a loss on the *where* to shop, so I tell him to take me to the West Farms Mall. I don't really like dresses, but because New York has been my obsession this year, I decide I'll get a black velvet dress. I wish I had some boots to wear with it, but we only have snow boots and practical clothes in our family. A dress for Christmas day is as boutique as it gets.

The mall is full of people, noise, and blaring Christmas music which feels jarring after our quiet, sullen house.

Everything is too much, the canned peppermint smell in the air, the department store perfume, the damp of winter coats, the overheated aisles filled with people sweating in their sweaters and scarves as they mash together. I feel exposed somehow. Dad lurking in the girls' department, his hands hanging helplessly at his sides doesn't help things. I work as quickly as I can, sliding the dresses on their plastic hangers along the rack, *snick, snick, snick*. I think we're both relieved when, mission accomplished, we head back to the car.

Dad takes me to Friendly's and we slide into a booth close enough to the front door that it's cool and I can leave my sweater on. He hasn't shaved in a few days and looks all kinds of worn out. The restaurant's quieter than the mall and the fried food smells get my stomach going. While I want a tuna melt, it's getting dark out and I'm suddenly anxious about getting home, so I order a strawberry Fribble and an order of fries.

Dad's doing that polite smile he usually saves for company and sits over his coffee, which feels more like a prop than something he actually wanted. After a spell of quiet, he says, "So, kiddo. How you feeling?"

And like that, the fact that Solstice is *tomorrow* comes flooding back to me with a stomach grip around my fries and shake. "I. I don't know."

He smiles. "I'm proud of you. You've been training hard. You're ready to step up and step in. We'll have so much to talk about come Wednesday."

"We can't talk about it now?" I said weakly.

He merely shoots me a look and goes on. "You'll be stepping into our centuries old traditions and your proper place in the world. Are you ready for that? To be a real Massey?"

The half a shake left in the glass suddenly becomes an impossibility, so I bob my straw up and down in it without looking at him. *Does this mean I'm not a Massey yet? And you married in, are you a real Massey?* But I say, "I'm ready."

He says, "Attagirl."

On Solstice, I wake up before it's even light out. I curse myself. I have to make it through the whole night tonight, and I can't do that if I'm up this early. I squeeze my eyes shut and try to get back to sleep when the wind kicks up, clattering the branches outside our window. I huff.

"Scared?" Martina's voice startles me out of the quiet dark.

"Terrified."

"Sucks."

This neither comforts nor confirms my feelings.

She sighs, saying, "Might as well get up. If you can catch a nap somewhere around two, it might set you up for the night. But no sense trying to sleep now."

"Tell me about your first time."

"No."

I laugh.

She does not.

I look up at the ceiling where a parallelogram of light shines orange from the streetlamp outside. As if I've commanded it by looking, it shifts and shines white as some headlights go past. It must be at least 5:30. It's a Tuesday. People will be going to work. People will be going to school. Our family always takes Solstice off, but the rest of the world will go on as usual. Nothing to see here. Nothing going on in the basement.

As if the house hears me, it sighs, a long, long exhale. My heart beats faster and anything I've imagined over the past eight years floods my brain--from technique to training, to imagining a giant hydra, a fiery dragon, an army of people, a blackness where I can't breathe. I dream up a sharp thing in the dark, like whatever got Carl that time.

Two left, stab right, slide forward. I clench my eyes

shut and try to blow my breathing which has come out in a gasp.

Martina says quickly, "Nuclear annihilation tomorrow. Today I will..." she thinks a moment, "Buy all of the ice cream at the corner store and eat it one spoon at a time, but only if you get the chips."

It's a game we used to play. My heart swells for her bringing it up. But I can't get a sudden new image of a pack of rats in the basement out of my head. Rats with swords.

Martina says, "You go."

"Nuclear annihilation tomorrow. I will..." I can't even form a thought. Those rats are poking me.

"Food, crush, or revenge." Martina has a steadiness in her voice, a guidance I usually only hear from Mama.

"Okay, revenge."

"Ooooh." She turns sideways to face me, although her figure is still dark.

"I will tell everyone I saw Kristen and Jimmy making out behind the school last year."

"And? Like don't most people already know that?"

She's right, there's no adequate revenge for bullies.

I say, "I'll smack them both wicked hard and finally tell them what I think."

"Attagirl."

"You sound like Dad." I drop my voice like his, "Attagirl."

"Well, I will beat them up for you if you need it. Nuclear annihilation or not."

"Uh. Thanks?" This camaraderie from Martina is unfamiliar.

Martina flops back on her bed. "Nuclear annihilation tomorrow I will tell Scott Cassella I am madly in love with him and I'll make out with him."

"Eeewwww."

"I might even..."

"Don't say it. Don't say it!" I squeal. This whole boys thing is not cool or fun. I don't know why she's so obsessed.

She says it anyway, "...go all the way."

"Duuude, you're like fifteen!"

"Sixteen next year and I don't want to die having never done it."

"Ice cream over that, any day. Okay my turn. Nuclear annihilation tomorrow and I will…"

We keep on like this until it's light out, and we make our way downstairs. The house is breathing steadily, like it's gearing up, just for me. Does it do this every year? Was it always this intense? The thin, blue sunlight comes in through the windows, leaving branch shadows on the walls. I haven't been afraid of the house like this before. It's our refuge, our home, our center, our place to hide out, to eat well, to have friends. It protects us from thunderstorms and rain and sheltered so many friends that January of the ice storm when we were the only ones in town with heat. But today is Solstice. We owe it something.

The humans in the house are quiet, but each one of us thrums with a silent tension. Everyone is getting weird. Martina gives me a huge squeezy hug for no reason when we're at breakfast. Jeffrey tousles my hair every time he passes me until I tell him to cut it out. Dad keeps catching me and patting me on the back like I'm a dog who's done something good. I wish they'd stop. All the differences in this day charge through my nerves and ratchet things up.

No training today, I'll need all my strength for tonight. Today I get sole possession of the best TV chair and my choice of television but since it's a weekday, it's only *I Love Lucy* and *I Dream of Jeannie*. No Sunday movies or anything. I turn on the soaps after lunch because of the drama music and the serious conversations. It all becomes blurred as I fall asleep.

I wake to a loud commercial playing an electronic version of the Carol of the Bells and the most Solsticey feeling ever, because the house is filled with the smell of pork roast and potatoes with a hint of rosemary. I was dreaming a springtime dream, perhaps because someone has put a fuzzy blanket over me and Gainsly is asleep on my feet.

I'm sweaty. But here I am, the sunlight already waning, it's getting time for dinner and it's my turn.

"Good morning, sleepyhead." Trust Dad to say the cliché dad thing. He's standing in the doorway and a part of me wonders if he hasn't been doing the stare at you until you wake up bit. "How you feeling?"

"Fine." Horrible. Terrified. Upset. Irritated that he's asking.

"Good, Good." Dad looks up to the frame on the wall, which is a very old, yellowed document with writing scrawled on it. He taps the frame, "Do you know what this is?"

"The deed. Yes."

"There was no one to draw it up because there wasn't even a town here yet. Your twelve times great grandfather had to mail it to England to make it official."

"And the land was ours. I got it."

He chuckles. "Well, kiddo, when you're all grown up and this place is yours, you can bore your own kids with that story."

Birthright. A quick flicker of excitement penetrates my fear. I kick Gainsly off my legs and heave myself off the sofa.

Mama stares at me as she serves the meal. Usually she's kinda absent, going through the motions, but there's definitely something new at play in her eyes this year. She stares at me to the point where it's creepy. I look right at her and say, "What?" I guess I said it too harshly because tears come to her eyes. She gets up from the table, walks over to me and gives me a hug, a kiss on the head, and she's out the door without a word. That anger that I felt when she bailed on Martina has turned to a feeling of complete betrayal and abandonment. She's leaving me to do this on my own. I swallow some tears I didn't expect.

Martina and Jeffrey look after her, stunned, without a word. Something is definitely off.

I have to ask Dad again, "Is there something you're not telling me? I mean aside from all the things you don't tell me?"

He picks up his whiskey and downs it in one gulp. He gets up and walks over to the cabinet above the stove where the whiskey bottle is stored and pours another. A tall one. The last time I saw him pour a second whiskey was after Carl came up with that cut. And that was like forever ago.

Jeffrey says, "Is Mama coming back? What about the cocoa?"

Martina scrambles and gets up, "I'll get it. Don't worry about Mama. She has a headache."

I say, "What are you not telling me?"

Jeffrey raises his eyebrows and shrugs. "Look, you'll know soon enough. Then we can talk."

Martina makes the cocoa and passes out three cups. Then she and Jeffrey start gearing me up and offering last minute advice.

As she pulls the breastplate over my head, Martina says, "Make sure to watch that left lunge, he..."

"*Martina*," Dad warns. He says to me. "The left is important, it's the one you don't see coming when you're fighting to the right. And whatever you do, don't look."

Jeffrey straps the shin guards on my legs. "Is this too tight?"

I push Dad, "I won't look, I mean, I know, I know. But what if I see something? I can't help my eyes."

Dad, who is shoring up the shoulders of my breastplate with safety pins stops suddenly and steps around in front of me so I can see him. His face is terrible, his voice is worse. "Shea, what have I taught you?"

I flush like I've been smacked. I look at the ground and murmur, "Watch your feet, remember the moves and you'll be okay."

"Right. If you remember everything we've taught you, you'll be fine."

The worry on his face totally freaks me out. "Daddy?"

He pulls me to him, and my breastplate hits him with a *thunk*. "I love you kiddo. You're brave. You got this." He murmurs this into my hair and his voice cracks which doesn't instill confidence, nor does the fact that I smell whiskey on him in a saturated way that lets me know he's been drinking it a while. This year, that drinking is heavy and it's about me. And he never hugged anyone else before they went down. It's off brand for prepping the kid for battle. My clattering heart jangles out to my limbs with a newfound panic. *Why is this all different?*

Martina and Jeffrey get the duct tape and fasten the flashlight to one of my hands, the crowbar to another. Even when I swear I will never drop my weapon, they insist this is the way things are done. I'm pushed and prodded and tightened. My chest hurts, and I want to cry but I just say, "Jeffrey, the right leg is too tight."

He kneels and adjusts it and then smacks my leg twice when he's done.

We walk around to the basement door together. I might just barf.

Dad lifts the 2 x 4 from across the door. They always said it was for burglars, but I know better. Dad turns on the light, a single bulb that hangs from the ceiling down below me.

I look back at my family. I swear Martina's gonna cry. Dad nods at me and I step down two stairs so they can close the door behind me. The door closes, leaving me in the breathing basement. The *kathunk* as they slide the bar back into place seals it. I am here. For the duration. They'll settle around the kitchen table drinking cocoa and tea until the night is done. Everything in me wishes I was on the other side of that door tonight.

This is my first time in the basement at night and my only time alone. It smells of dirt floor with an undertone of oily singed furnace. I've only ever been down here in the summer with Martina for tools, or, on the hottest days with Jeffrey, to sit on the cool stairs eating Doritos and drinking soda. No one ever comes down here at night and Dad puts that bar over the door each sunset to remind us.

I hate these stairs. They are wood, and have a railing, but there are no backs to their risers. It's only ever dark blackness at your feet with the unknown space behind. Anything could reach through and grab your ankles. I get a creepy feeling around my legs like a million cockroaches, but I stand still an extra moment. Normally I'd scramble down to the bottom, closer to the ground, safer. But tonight, the house is breathing heavily, and I'm inside that breath. A million cockroaches beat whatever's waiting for me down there in the dark.

The house sucks in a furnace-deep breath and there's a clank and it exhales a sigh. I know I have to get in position, ready to start, or it will get the advantage. I grip the poker in one hand, try not to sweat too much on the flashlight, and start down the stairs, unsteady as I haven't any hands to hold the rail. I go one step at a time, preschool style. I breathe, whispering, "Remember," into the empty space. *Scuff, step,* "Remember." *Scuff, step,* "Don't look."

When I get to the bottom, the earthen floor is so cold it stings. How can anything be so cold underground? It's like walking on an icy sidewalk in rubber rain boots. I turn around and walk into the pitch black of the back of the basement.

In summer I asked Dad why we couldn't have a light in the darkest part of the basement. He said we just can't. When I badgered Martina on the topic, she just shook her head and said, "Solstice."

The space feels, sounds? Smells? Bigger somehow. Bigger than the basement ever was. Cavernous.

I scuff my feet along the dirt floor and the furnace kicks in. There's a loud clatter to my left and I swerve and stab a bunch of paint cans on the shelves that run along the wall, turning the clatter into a deluge of metal and thuds. I move my feet quickly so they don't get crushed. My flashlight hit the cans in the first place, but the poker is what brought them down. Fortunately, most of the cans are only half full. One of them cracks open and an eggy vinegar spoiled paint odor insinuates itself through everything. I stand for a moment, heart pounding, wondering what my family upstairs has made of the noise.

I slow my breath and flash my flashlight forward, peering into the darkness.

The "don't look" has a lot of questions and answers and explanations. But long and short, I'm supposed to look to find my way, but not stare at what I might see.

I slide my feet along the ground again, just like I was taught. The dirt floor scuffs up its own smell, but something else replaces it. The basement smells are supplanted by a thick, ugly animal odor. This is a reptile smell, like the stink of the lizard tank my friend Kevin had...only if you took that stink to the tenth power. As swiftly as the odor changes, the floor does too, and my foot hits something solid, but fleshy. I whisk my flashlight down to reveal a frighteningly pale, fleshy mass with reptilian skin. Like a tentacle without suckers? Like a tree root, but soft. The skin is a muted whiteness with yellowing pinkish hues rippling through its surface. I nudge it with my foot again when a grumble wakes deep in the darkness and grows. My own gasp startles me, and I carefully pick my way over the...arm? Tentacle? Tree growth? I move my way in forward, sliding my feet. See, mystery solved. Now I know why we slide our feet. Why couldn't they just tell me, "You will encounter a fleshy sort of thing..." Why the big mystery? Why only the moves? Couldn't they have better prepared us?

The groan grows in volume and turns into a growl. I remember my sibs have all done this and everyone knows Jeffrey's a pussy. I trained for this. I squint into the darkness and flash the flashlight to the left twice, thrust the poker forward. I've got this.

Something red glows awake in the far back of the

blackness. The furnace? I squint to see it, and just make something out when I'm hit from the left side by a massive force of cold pale flesh. *Watch out for your left side.* I stumble sideways and fall onto the same cold, hard but fleshy substance. I yelp and scramble to my feet stabbing the air in front of me with the poker. I hit soft flesh and there is a sudden roar of anger from the beast.

I swipe the flashlight to the right, three times as I was taught, and stab left with the poker. Hit flesh. The rhythm comes naturally, has been trained into me. But nothing can prepare me for stabbing something alive. Even if it isn't human. I yelp, but go back to counting.

One, two, stab, stab, advance. One, oh shit. Stab. Forgot two. Two.

Whump

Hit from the entirely opposite side with a thunk so hard I see stars, I go over again. The hit is concussive, and I wonder what could have possibly gotten Carl those years back when he needed stitches. Maybe I just haven't gotten to the sharp part yet.

The roaring is merely in reaction to the stabs that make contact, but the growl rises steadily to a level that hurts. A level that makes me think I am somehow in the beast now.

Swipe with the flashlight two times. Don't look. But the flashlight catches the hideous hugeness of a full wall of this beast. And there's something stuck in the back wall where the redness is coming from. Is that a piece of plastic stuck up there on the whitish walls?

Don't look. You have to promise me you will not look. I can see the anxiousness on Mama's face when she told me this. Her insistence.

I look at my feet and swish the flashlight two to the left, stab forward, advance.

Roar. Piercing shriek, breathing.

I wonder at hearing the living, close-up part of the distant noises I've heard only through the floor over the years. The cocoa, the kitchen table, the roars and clanks below, muffled, distant, but harrowing. Now here they are, live, real, inescapable. I'm a part of those noises now. Whatever this is.

The furnace switches on and glows from an entirely different space from where I thought it was. Off to the left. That means the red glow ahead of me is no furnace. I swallow.

Swipe two to the left, poke right, advance.

I'm supposed to stop advancing and reach my standoff soon. It has to be soon. As soon as my feet meet something higher than the floor. They said it would be solid. They said it would be cold. They never said it would be flesh. Once I can't slide past that place, I'm meant to stand. And not look. And to hold it back with the very moves with which I advanced on it. To hold it back until the dawn.

Swipe, swipe, poke, advance. I'm still advancing well past where our basement is supposed to end. Surely, I've walked the length of the front of the house, if not another entire block.

Two more cycles and I hit it. I nose my toe to the right, along the edge. To the left along the edge. It's impassable. It's not an arm, tentacle, whatever, it's the solid form of itself.

And then you stand. And you look at the floor. And you swipe and poke, at a steady rate of one cycle every two minutes. This is when it gets quiet. But this is when it gets harder. Whatever you do, do not look.

I've trained for this. I'm prepared. I'm ready.

The thing is, the two minutes take forever to pass. I stare at my digital watch to keep track.

The breathing is louder than I've ever heard it before. It's all around me and this creature is so enormous, it's not all in the room with me. It seems like this is the small edge of something more massive than I can imagine. Maybe more massive than anyone knows. The breathing vibrates in the earth beneath my feet, shudders in the walls that slope up either side of me.

And whatever you do, do not speak to it. It will say anything to get you on its side.

"Let me go." The voice doesn't match the breathing. It's a small voice, like from a person. A very sad, exhausted sort of person.

I'm not supposed to listen. I swipe the flashlight and stab and stare at the blackness beneath me.

"I can't do this anymore, please let me go." Not only is the voice small, it's young. Young like a teenager?

Do not look.

"Shea? Is that you?" It says.

They never said it would know my name.

"You're the youngest. Aren't you? Like Mama and Dad didn't go have a sixth kid, did they?"

I know I'm not supposed to, but I look. My flashlight shines on the back wall of the basement and on the undulating fleshy whiteness that drapes out into the darkness behind it, there are chunky black glasses stuck into the wall. The glasses are fused to a face of human flesh, colored in the peachy tawniness of our family. Flat blue, tired eyes gaze out at me.

It's Toby.

The noise that comes out of me takes the shape of an "oh," but is half moan and all cry.

It's Toby, but not. His face is still colored like ours, but the white flesh starts around the rim of his hairline and goes back into the shadowed pale walls and the creature. The red glow is a pulsating light in the rippling pallid flesh far enough below his face it's where his heart would be. The red glow sits in a human length lump of reptilian flesh where the rest of his body should be. But it's not human shaped, that lump. Not really.

My moan lets loose the tears and I say, "I don't understand."

"It'll be your firstborn, too, you know." When he turns his head, the flesh around it quivers outward. He isn't trapped in it, so much as part of it.

I think of Mama and how we aren't allowed to mention Toby. The tears come in gulps now. "I don't..."

"The firstborn of the lastborn. I feed the house. I feed the happiness. I hold back..." his eyes flash a deeper glowing red and the voice that groaned awake echoes through the being, "...this thing."

"How could she let you?" *Did she give him to it? Does she know? Of course she knows. This is why she won't let us talk about Toby. Jesus. How does she send her kids down into this every year?*

He smiles dully. "It's just how things are done."

"What happens if you aren't here to hold it back?"

"It won't work for us. It'll get out of control. It's most powerful on Solstice, feeding off the dark and the cold. That's why I need help today."

"What is it?"

He doesn't answer. He breathes deep and the walls around him shudder with it. "You'll be asked to say an oath when you go back upstairs. They'll let you rest first and then tomorrow, you'll say the oath. You'll be asked to become part of this."

"But we've always lived here. We've always fought this." *This means that Martina knows? Jeffrey knows? Is this why Carl won't come home anymore?*

"You're the youngest. Mama was the youngest. It'll be your firstborn." *Maybe this is why Mama is so hard this year. So...closed off. She knows I'm the youngest. Which means what again? It means I get the house but is this the price?*

Toby says, "Honestly, I can't wait to be released."

"I don't. Released?"

"Your two minutes..."

I look at my watch. He's right. But now. I can't.

He insists, "They'll expect it."

Swipe, Swipe, stab. The poker barely touches his trunk, but he lets loose a roar of anger and indignation that make me stab an extra time, hitting flesh.

"That's right. That's the way to do it." He sounds tired. So tired.

"Did you talk to Carl? To Jeffrey? To Martina?"

"Carl is the only one who listened."

"Carl is the only one who left."

The house sighs. Toby sighs. It's one; it's double, but the sigh is large and vibrates the house around me. "I don't blame him really. He was older. What's there to lose? He couldn't live with it. And he had a choice," he added. Was that bitterness? He sighed again and I thought of all the times the house had sighed. Was it really Toby sighing? He said, "Carl really loved you, you know."

This hits me in the chest and the lump wells up in my throat again. So much of every part of my life is tangled up in this and I can't make sense of the new patterns. Each thread thrums through years of information. Carl left, but Carl loved me. Mama knows about me as youngest. Mama gave up her firstborn kid. Dad has known about this all along. Martina and Jeffrey know and are okay with it. They are okay with it and Carl was not. Carl left. Carl loved me.

I say, "I miss him."

His laugh strangles in a growl and he says, "I do too. He was the only one who really talked to me. Until now."

Tears come to my throat and my voice chokes. "Mama let this happen to you."

The flesh around him is rumbling, rippling, pushing forward.

Toby says, "Two minutes."

I can barely lift the poker, but I swipe and stab. It roars, he roars, but the rumbling recedes.

I said, "I don't understand why."

"It feeds this."

"But what *is* it?"

All of the noise stops for a moment as if the entire being is contemplating the question. The house breathes really really deep and Toby says. "It's something our ancestors brought over. I know that. On the boats. Waaay back."

"But why our family?"

"I don't know. And I don't know if we're the only ones. I do know our country wouldn't be what it is without it. It's a hunger. A need. A power. It got us here alive. It killed off the Indians. It grew with land theft. It grew with slavery, it grew into manifest destiny. It grew with railroads and money and stocks and greed. It grew with erasure. It made our people...what they are." He says the last line bitterly.

Our people. I don't know what that means. "But that's not. That's not *us*. That's, like ancestor crap." I know about smallpox. I know about slavery. But this is 1978. We're free to be you and me, we had the Bicentennial, our country is freedom, liberty for all, Sesame Street, women's lib.

"We live here. This is our ancestors. This is us. Two minutes."

It takes me a moment to process, but the rumble starts again, and I swipe, stab, Toby roars and we are quiet.

After a minute, I say, "The deed. We've owned this place forever."

Toby's laugh, one "ha" is reiterated in the gut of the beast, resonating. "Own. That's your problem right there."

I will have a kid one day, and that kid will have to do this. For. The house? I inherit the house because I'm the youngest. Mama knows this. When did she tell Dad this? Did he know when they were married? Did he know when they first had Toby?

"Why? How do we make it stop?"

And Toby starts talking long and low with two minute intervals of action/reaction as we fight the beast and work it through.

We go on like this until morning. Talking in the two minutes between. Trying to figure a way out of it. It might be as simple as the freeze that's coming in two days. It will definitely ruin Christmas, but it's the only way out. And I can't do this. I can't be part of this. And I can't run like Carl, knowing Toby is down here. Stuck. Knowing that the whole family is still doing this. Every year. And knowing what it started, all of this. And what might it bring?

I don't even know if I want kids, but I can't have this at the other end of that decision.

I can't.

The dawn comes. I tell Toby I love him. I mean it in a fierce, protective way I only felt about Carl and Martina before I knew she knew. Yesterday. That thought makes me so tired.

Toby goes to sleep. His eyes close, the red glow inside the pale flesh fades and the fleshiness takes him in, first creeping up and covering his face and his glasses, then folding over him and receding back into the shadows in the basement. I sit down and just start blubbering. I imagine, aside from that first meltdown when he first told me, I was being strong for him all those hours. And we have a plan now, but I have to go back up to face that family who knows about this, to that family that was okay with this. I loved them so much, but it's like that love has been replaced with a giant black hole of anger and disappointment. It's too much.

I try to slow my breathing and get the blubbering under control. Did Martina cry? I do this trick Mama taught me to stop the crying: you recite "The Owl and the Pussycat" in your head until your breathing comes under control.

All these years. I forgot to ask him how time moves for him. Is it the same as us? Does he spend minute after minute in the darkness until the next Solstice?

Not this time.

I get to my feet and make my way up the stairs as slowly as I'd come down them, my knees weary, my poker and flashlight impossibly heavy. The poker smacks each step as I can't even raise that arm anymore. *Step, clunk, step, clunk.* I raise my flashlight hand enough to knock on the door once and I hear Dad lift the bar from the other side. I gulp back my tears. I'm not ready to talk to anyone about this yet. I'm not prepared to create even the false story that

I'm part of this. I mostly want bed. Did Carl cry, too?

They are all standing on the other side of the door looking at me anxiously.

Well, most of them. Mama isn't there. For the first Solstice ever, she stayed in bed. I wonder if it's because she knows. The last born's first born... She knows, remembers herself at that age. She knows what it means.

Martina says, "How was it?"

Dad says with some ridiculous relief in his voice, "Well, now everyone knows, no more secrets."

Jeffrey says, "You okay?"

They don't look the same to me. I hate their faces. All of them.

I say, "But why?" This stops them. And I cough. *Has no one asked this question before?*

Dad says, "It's. It's a hard truth, honey. It's just the way things work around here."

"But why can't we stop it?"

Martina makes an *oooh* noise like I'm in trouble.

Dad sighs. "Go to bed honey. It'll make more sense after you've slept some. It's a lot to take in. Especially for you."

I eat a piece of cold apple pie they've left out for me and drink a big glass of milk and then I head up the stairs to bed. *When did this house get so many stairs? This house.* An ache and weakness shakes each leg as I pull it up another step. Everything is heavy now.

I sleep until noon the following day. I wake up with a sour mouth, a splitting headache, and a determination to end this nonsense. Martina is gone. I reach over and grab the aspirin and water waiting for me on my bedside table. The solution is simple, really. And if no one else is going to help Toby, I will.

When I go downstairs, Dad's in his study working the jigsaw puzzle he started at Thanksgiving. It's some ridiculously hard to decipher jungle scene, but I think on his non-drinking days it's how Dad makes it to Solstice. He's almost done, which is just as well because present wrapping will take over this area shortly. He's whistling, that heavy cloud of Solstice lifted. It was always a relief to see this in him, but now it feels sinister.

I don't want to even have to deal with him, but I'm expected to check in and have a talk. I can't remember ever wanting to completely avoid Dad, aside from maybe after our weird sex talk two years before. But this isn't that kind of avoidance. I can't stand the idea of him. All of the conversations we've had around Solstice are rushing back through my head for their hidden meaning. And what felt like his caring, his supporting me, his "attagirl," is really something so terrible I can't sort it yet.

He's bent over the puzzle so far I can see his little round bald patch, and when I see his hunched shoulders, his hand paused with a puzzle piece hovering over the table, I want to start yelling, raging at him. I want to go back to yesterday when I believed he only wanted the best for his children. Back to the him I really loved. I want to burst out crying. Instead, I clear my throat.

"Hey kiddo!" He's cheerful. *What the hell?*

I say, "So I gotta do an oath or something?"

He stands up rubbing his palms on his legs as he does so. He says, "Yes, yes, let me see." And he goes around to behind Grandpa Massey's desk, opening the drawer with his key. I never even thought Mama and Dad locked things up. I wonder what Grandpa locked up in there.

Grandpa, who knew when he sent Mama down. The awfulness of all of this layers back through everything I loved about this place.

My birthright.

This house may only go back to 1902, but Mama's family has lived on this property in one form or another since they moved here in 1603. I start to think the basement predates the house. I start thinking of oldests and youngests in mobcaps, in britches, with muskets. I wonder if The Wangunk lived here before and if the basement was like that then. But Toby said our family brought this here. This horror. Is it the sort of thing you dig a hole for and plant? Is this a space where something bad happened and it's haunted?

This land belonged to the Wangunk tribe before. Not like "belonging" was something they really thought about land. But whatever my ancestors brought started here. And grew.

Dad pulls out a piece of paper that's yellow and thick like a page from one of our super old Oz books. He hands it to me. I take it carefully. It's in weird old timey English and Dad says, "the Fs are Ss." I tremble it out pronouncing as best I can. It has so many therebys and heretofores and flowery language I can barely parse it, so maybe that makes it easier. Something about holding back evil. *Yeah with Toby.* Something about recompensing for something and claiming and protecting the land and of course, something about silence until death.

I cross my fingers the whole time.

Protect the land. It's not our land, is it? If you really think about it. And the house will go to me. So we can keep this shit going on for more generations.

When I finish it an, "Amen," comes out before I think to stop it and Dad chuckles. I keep my eyes to the ground because if I look up he'll read what utter bullshit I found that. I say, "Uh. Thanks. Okay."

Dad lays his hand on my shoulder which only reminds me how sore my muscles are from the battle. He says, "I'm proud of you honey. I'm glad we can share all of *this* with you now," his arms go wide motioning around the great wild room, the slave ship on the mantelpiece—why didn't I ever think that was weird before? I knew it was a slave ship. The ancient desk, the deed, the old books, the house itself. Dad's domain. Our domain. Our inheritance.

His hands float back to my shoulders. "Now, do you have any questions?"

I gauge my response. What does Dad expect the prior

me to do? To say? But I can't. I don't have the energy to fake anything. I look up only then and say, "Dad, can I just take a day or two? I'm worn out."

I wait as he decides whatever and his face goes from eager to dead and his tone joins it. "Of course you can."

I can't help but feel I've disappointed him somehow and my first impulse is to say something to make the light come back in his eyes. He was so enthused just a moment ago. What does he need from me now? Were any of the others overjoyed about that awfulness in the basement?

Like all of the other lies in my life, I count on my Dad's unconditional love for me. I count on how much he validates me as a person, how he sees me and supports me, be it with homework or art supplies or books I'd like to read. I count on the quiet company we keep, the trips to the hardware store, the grocery, the Pizza Palace, the way he called me peanut when I was very small and then kiddo later with the same amount of love. But now it all feels like he was grooming me so he could hold on to this giant desk and this den, his ship's model, and his jigsaw puzzles. He loves this more than he loves me. He loves this more than he loves his firstborn son. Did he marry Mama knowing all this or did she break him in slowly?

Only a year ago, Dad said, "I married this house," in a pleased way that made me feel cozy and comfortable but that now echoes back with a chilling meaning.

But Toby and I have a plan. And I can't do anything about it for two days, anyway. Right now is my last day with full television privileges, so I do as expected, grab the remote from Jeffrey and stare at *Bewitched* while I try to sort things out. As long as I stay glued to the tube, maybe no one will try to talk to me.

The weather forecast foretold a cold snap, but when it hits, the temperatures plunge below what anyone expected. What was meant to bottom out around eleven degrees is going to get to negative two. A twenty-year record.

I walk around the house one last time that night, lingering in the kitchen, remembering summers before, when I didn't know. I take in bright yellow walls of the kitchen and the wood of the table, Gainsly's snuffle as he roots for incidental crumbs or bits of something from dinner. I feel a gaping sadness, not for the fact that this won't be here anymore, but for the fact that it's already lost to me. None of it means what I thought it did. I wander in through the dining room. The big top is still on the table from Thanksgiving so we can have Christmas there. We put the small round top back on the table after the holidays have gone. Two china closets stand sentry on the opposite door from the dining room. One was inherited from Dad's mom, one has always been here, and both are laden with generations of china, from Wedgewood to Royal Minten. Federalist silver, real Revereware. I used to stare at these treasures thinking of their history, their meaning to the family as each new generation married and treasures were passed down, added on. Now they loom, heavy with generations of knowing. The family pictures hang scattered on the wall of the front hall, all without Toby. Goofy pictures of me and Jeffrey in the back yard, sweaty from the summer, of Martina and me in matching dresses. What did Toby do those summers? Did he know they were passing?

I'm getting maudlin. No one will be hurt. It's just a stupid house with a bad secret. And then it will be over. I'm not sure how I'll deal with my folks after but who knows, maybe breaking out of this awful Solstice cycle will free Mama. No more black moods.

It will free Toby, and that's what matters.

I kiss Mama goodnight that night for the first time since Solstice. This time I mean it. It's an *I'll take care of you* promise kiss. It's an ending the cycle kiss. It's a kiss for everything she's carried. I try not to think about what it means to give up one's firstborn. She goes *mmmmm* and throws her arm around me squeezing. She then turns back to her knitting. A scarf for someone for Christmas. Mama's always knitting and we never know who it's for. The surprise will be who opens the package with the cornflower blue scarf inside. But not this year, I guess.

I kiss Dad in a cursory way because I'm not really talking to him yet. Mama doesn't have much of a choice, but he joined this lie. Out of love for her? When did he know he'd have to give up Toby? Before they were married or after he had him? Or has he always been that way? I wonder how Mama and Dad treated Toby, were they assholes to him so he'd be an asshole and it would be easier? Or did they give him a ton of love because they knew what he'd have to carry?

I poke my head in Jeffrey's room where he's tooling with his guitar. He looks up and noses a greeting. I say, "Good night," and turn to go.

It's just me and Toby now.

We wait until everyone is asleep. We creep up the stairs into the attic in what used to be Toby's bedroom. Toby before. Toby the boy. It's now filled with boxes of things, cast off chairs, a walker from when Gram had her hip replaced. Gram knew too, what Solstice meant. She sacrificed a child. She knew her oldest grandson would be sacrificed. Gram of the homemade cinnamon buns and backyard golfing tee. Gram of the late-night fairy tales.

We fight our way through the stuff to the radiator. We turn the knob until it turns off and make our way back through the ocean of cardboard to the other side of the room and the bathroom. We go to the sink that stands next to that clawfoot tub where we took long soaks after Mama told us the truth, what we had to do. After she told us what we needed to sacrifice for the sake of the family. Before we went into the cold forever. Mama held our shoulder that time, led us down the stairs, into the back and even when we said, *no, no you can't make me*, she did, and she handed us over as the flesh surrounded us. The squelching sound as the monster released her oldest sister, our aunt, the roaring sound as it stretched to pull us in, It was so loud we didn't even hear if she cried for us. Did she cry? Did she ever even love us?

And we are fixing this now. No one should have to do this again. We'll both be free. We are unwinterizing in winter. The cold snap is coming tonight, and it will do the work for us. We turn on the water pipe to the attic bathroom. The water will flow into that pipe, it will be too cold up here from the snap and if we work from the basement and the attic, it will go more quickly.

Here in the basement, we know our powers. We know our powers to hold back, but also to let go a little. It hates the furnace; the furnace is warmth and light. It can't wait to get to it. We let go a little and it swells and grows, filling the basement, thrilled to be given its limbs. Nothing to fight back here, our wills are united as we stretch and stretch until the flesh reaches the furnace. This is what the parents didn't tell us for the fighting: we mustn't let it reach the furnace. We followed orders, not knowing what we were fighting back. But without me to hold it in place, we grow up around the furnace and it is hot, and we don't like it, but we don't care, for soon we will all be free.

What's a little pain in the face of a lifetime? We are weak after Solstice, they never explained to us that we'd work together, the siblings. That was our sacrifice. Working to fight back the cold, then only one of us gets to go upstairs to life again.

No one else will have to do this again, that's for sure.

The pain is certainly no more than being fought back, but there is sizzling, a bit of smoke. In five seconds without oxygen, the fire is snuffed and the burning stops. Time and cold will do their work now. We will soon be free.

We bleed the radiator in the attic room so it also floods with water. Who knows the pipe that will burst first?

We go to bed as instructed and wait. Somewhere in the middle of the night, when we have just dozed off, there is a distant clank from the attic bathroom and the water begins to flow. We grab our bag of stuff and move downstairs. We listen outside our door to the hallway where the family sleeps, but there is no noise at all aside from Mama's snore that matches the breathing of the house. You would have to work hard to hear that water.

Soon. Soon we will be released from this. All of us will be released.

Then there is a clank from the bathroom on the second floor.

Unlike with fire, no one will be hurt. All of us can get out in time. And this will finally be over.

I wait in the front hall at the bottom of the stairs until a trickle creeps into a cold wet patch on my leg and I stand. The stairwell is becoming a waterfall, slowly, like when you first turn the hose on the Slip 'n Slide. Four more clanks and the trickle turns into a rush, and an actual waterfall is in place when a door bursts open upstairs and I hear Dad, "What the fuck is going on here?" Dad's not a swearer.

As if he'd willed it, that is the moment the water, pooling on the floor of the upstairs hallway starts sheeting down off the edge of the floor where it meets the bannister, like on Pirates of the Caribbean, making Dad's consequent yells distant and warbly as it creates a barrier over the stairwell.

I take my bag and wait by the front door. I watch the water sheet over the stairwell, the mini waterfall on the last curve of the landing as the smells and presence of the house change from dry warmth, food and books, to wet wool, soaking antiques, metallic flow and water, water. The sheet of water is colored as the sun rises behind the stained-glass window. I loved that window. But we are saving Toby, so anything we're doing is worth it. We're saving any child I might have one day.

It's a full ten minutes before my family walks through that sheet of water, like they're coming from another dimension. My Dad first, wet, bedraggled, his eyes fall on me, waiting there and relief crosses his face. He hollers back through the barrier to another world, "I found her!" He's soaking wet. Jeffrey follows, then Mama, then finally with a grand noisy smatter because she had the brains to use an umbrella. Then Martina.

Dad says, "What are you waiting for, open the door!"

As I open it, there's an enormous creaking and crash upstairs, shaking the house followed by a house-wide moan that I worry is Toby. Something has fallen or shifted. We all look back, incredulous as the stream of water coming down the stairwell turns into a flood. There's a creaking and groaning underlying the mad sound of rushing water and Dad herds us outside into the sparkling cold. I had prepared, putting the spare blankets from the TV room on the curb. I hand them to Martina and Jeffrey who take them without question and Mama whose brow furrows and Dad who snatches it, throws it around his shoulders and runs next door. Likely to find a phone.

After a long minute, Mama says, "Shea..."

But then Dad comes running back toward us. "Half an hour."

Mama says, "Half an hour, look at it!"

Water is flooding out the front door, as it was meant to, but there is something shifting in the house. Is it off plumb, or has it always been that way because of the hill? It creaks and groans as something larger shifts and falls inside.

By the time the water company gets there to turn off the main, it has definitely started listing to the left down the hill. Water is pouring out from between the clapboards on the second floor. The man from the city is older with an orange stocking cap pulled down over his ears under his white helmet. He jumps back in his truck and fetches a long metal tong-like thing. He looks up at the house disbelieving and my Dad coughs to shake him out of it. He clears his throat, pops the lid off a cover in the ground and twists the main shut.

We all look back at the house. I wonder if Toby drowned.

I wonder where we will move, how this will change everything. How pissed Mama will be when she learns the truth. Or will she maybe be relieved? To be released from this cycle? I imagine us all living in an apartment in town. Life containable, conquerable. We can still do all our regular city stuff, Pizza Palace, trips to the shops on Main Street to see the decorations. But it will be just us. Without the house. The history. The weight. Dad's job can afford an apartment. I only have five more years before I get out of here anyway. Maybe I can look up Carl and he'll let me move in with him. I'll get a job. We'll be fine. And without all that time training in winter, who knows what we can do?

We watch, but it takes a few moments for the water to slow at all. Once it does, as if water were the only thing holding it together, the listing turns into real movement and the house goes completely crooked, sliding off of and into its foundation. The roof, once proud and arched, caves in on itself. Glass shatters, beams break, and it falls. It sighs as it does so. There is this sense of...release.

Toby is free.

I'm free.

My kid is free.

My family is free.

I smile.

Mama says, "Shea..."

I turn to her saying, "It's over, Mama. All done. We don't have to do this anymore."

I can feel Jeffrey and Martina turning to face me, but I don't take my eyes off Mama.

Dad says, "Shea, honey." The endearment has turned to acid.

Mama says, "What did you do?" in such a poisonous voice I don't think I've ever heard before.

"I set Toby free. I set all of us..." but my confidence fades as her face moves from fury to sadness to fear.

"We were the guardians."

"Of the house, I know."

Mama collapses onto the lawn, her legs splayed funny, her fuzzy bunny jammy pants a stark pink against the dead grass. She sobs, "No, no, no, no, no, no."

"Mama?"

Dad starts in, "Jesus Christ, Shea, did you think about consulting with any of us before you made this enormous decision for the family?"

"Mama?"

She looks up at Dad and swallows. "We have to go. Now." She turns to me and says, "It's not Toby you freed honey. You freed it."

She looks back at the house. The water has slowed to a trickle running down the sidewalk. The bright yellow wood of the outside of the house is mixed with the dark wood of the inside, and both are mixed with something pale and terrifying. It's then that I see them, the reaching fronds, the branches of white flesh. Growing out from the house's front, reaching, stretching across the yard. Toward us? Toward everything.

SPRING

MARTINA

She didn't want the house? Fine. But she didn't have to fucking ruin everything just because she wussed out of her family duty.

Worked out in the end. I mean, Dad had to get Jeffrey down there tout suite. I told Dad they should really go and fetch Carl, but he said there wasn't time and Carl was a grown man now and might very well not come. Jeffrey blubbered and whimpered, and Shea tried to throw her skinny ass between them, but she slipped on the ice and went down. She was screaming and crying and her voice was so thin in the morning air. Mama just sat there next to the fire hydrant on the parkway, wrapped in a blanket and shaking her head while Dad stormed up the front stairs holding Jeffrey by the upper arm. Jeffrey skidded on the ice, but Dad held him upright with more strength than I knew he had.

Top of the porch was hard to figure with the house a pile of roofing and clapboard and wood and crap. Dad stood there, Jeffrey wailing, "no..." Everyone knows Jeffrey's a pussy.

The house knew what to do. Or the thing. Because this house was kaput, Shea made sure of that. It was so fast. Dad standing there, Jeffrey wailing and then these filthy white fleshy limbs, pinkish in the morning light, snatched Jeffrey by the ankles, wound up around his chest and pulled him down so fast it surprised his wail into stopping. There was a sucking noise and the ground trembled as it settled beneath us. The white roots that had formed in the yard pulled themselves back down and disappeared under the torn up grass and dirt.

They sent Shea to Choate. *Boarding* school. I'd be jealous and all, but this means I get the house. I know what you're thinking, I mean, you saw what happened. But this happens every once in a while. Some family member wants to be a hero. Wants to make it stop. Wants to share the wealth and comes up with some melting pot bullshit. Some equality for all line. We all know how this works, how it's been working since our ancestors first landed and took the land that was destined for them.

We nurture this thing that we brought here, that gave us all of this. And we enjoy the fruits of our labor, sea to shining sea.

The last person who pulled a Shea was great Uncle Joe who wrote bad poetry, burned down the house, and then went off to college. That was 1901.

But the fun part is now, when we rebuild, I tell them what what I want. Mama's excited for me. But with Jeffrey in the basement and Carl gone and Shea not trustworthy, it's gonna be me down there battling that thing every year. So I want one of those House & Garden ultra-modern specials, big glass windows, travertine floors you could roller skate on and a hooded fireplace in the center of a giant living room. I want a conversation pit.

Maybe we can have a pool.

ABOUT THE AUTHOR

Kate Maruyama's first novel was *Harrowgate* (47North, 2013). Her short works have appeared in *Asimov's, Controlled Burn*, and *Stoneboat*; on *Entropy, Duende, The Rumpus, Salon* and other journals; as well as in numerous anthologies, including *Winter Horror Days* (Omnium Gatherum Media, 2015) and *Halloween Carnival 3* (Hydra, 2017).

Maruyama edited Nicole Sconiers's speculative short fiction collection, *Escape from Beckyville: Tales of Race, Hair and Rage* (Spring Lane Publishing, 2011), has been a jury chair for the Bram Stoker Awards and was twice a juror for the Shirley Jackson Awards. She is on the Diverse Works Inclusion Committee for the HWA. She teaches at Antioch University Los Angeles in the BA program and in their continuing education program, as well as for Los Angeles Writing Classes. She writes, teaches, cooks, and eats in Los Angeles, where she lives with her family.

ACKNOWLEDGMENTS

Thanks to Lisa Morton and Ellen Datlow, who inadvertently gave me the writing prompt for this book; their constant work in the field of horror is a daily inspiration to me.

To the Art, Tacos, Fiction (and Poetry!) San Clam gang for being amazing company, for their quiet creative energy and a gorgeous weekend where I could get my teeth into the thing. A special thanks to Xochitl Julisa-Bermejo and Rocìo Carlos for their fierce views, their openness and the way they check me and make me think harder about what I put out in the world. And to Kendra and Gen Maruyama, for their constant and generous loan of that creative space. To my writing fam, too large and gorgeous to name in one place, especially my constant readers, Toni Ann Johnson, Nicole D. Sconiers, Andromeda Romano Lax, Heather Luby, Yuvi Zalkow, and Seth Fischer, as well as my larger conversation writer fam, Chiwan Choi, David Davis, Natashia Deon, Traci Akemi Kato-Kiriyama, Maggie Downs, Lisa Morton, Cecil Castellucci, and the always inspiring ladies of Women Who Submit.

To my parents who always stood up to and fought against the inequities they saw about them in the workplace or in life in general. At the time, they were radical for flying in the face of the system from which they benefitted, when everyone looked at them like they were crazy or accused them of being pains in the ass. To them it was common sense. Shea is for them. My apologies to them and those who love the place for nestling systemic evil in our basement, but 45 Lawn was too awesome not to write about and its destruction too gothic.

Thanks to my brothers for tormenting me with Pinkeltein, the long lost made up brother who made me feel there was always someone missing at Thanksgiving. He was the inspiration for Toby, and a bit for Carl.

Thanks to my agent, John Silbersack, for supporting everything I do, even when there's no big payoff.

Thanks to my constant companion, Ko, especially for seeing me through the path of destruction of my childhood home that inspired this story. My parents and that house would have taken me with them if it weren't for his unconditional care, common sense, and his ability to make me laugh.

Thanks to Reed, my one-woman hype man and Jack, my mellowest companion in these trying times. They both have taught me more than they know and have made me a better person.

And the biggest thanks to Kate the First, my incredible editor Kate Jonez for her mad skills, friendship, vision, and support; and for shepherding this little book into the world. She is quietly making the world a better place.

Made in the USA
Middletown, DE
13 February 2021